GRAY FOX WALKS

by ISAAC PETERSON
and RUBY PETERSON   2013

Gray fox walks

so lightly

through

the woods .

The breeze moves slightly.

Autumn

leaves

fall.

Gray fox looks up

at the sky.

The moon is caught

in the
branches.

Gray fox sees

the river unwind
between
the
trees.

The water reflects
fox's eyes.

All the world is still

until

gray fox moves

again.

The path

bends

back.

She runs swiftly.

She leaps the log.

Back again

to her den.

Where her kits
are dreaming.

Fall asleep fox.

About the Authors

Isaac Peterson grew up in Alaska and loves comics, painting and photography. Ruby Peterson, his daughter, drew or painted many of the background elements in this book. Isaac and Ruby love working on projects together. We would love to hear from you! please write:

isaac.d.peterson@gmail.com
www.isaacpeterson.com

Made in the USA
Columbia, SC
28 September 2019